PIRATE TREASURE

Illustrated by Jim Durk

A GOLDEN BOOK · NEW YORK

Thomas the Tank Engine & Friends™

CREATED BY BRITT ALLCROFT

Based on The Railway Series by The Reverend W Awdry.
© 2015 Gullane (Thomas) LLC.
Thomas the Tank Engine & Friends and Thomas & Friends are trademarks of Gullane (Thomas) Limited.
HIT and the HIT Entertainment logo are trademarks of HIT Entertainment Limited.
ISBN 978-0-553-52478-9
randomhousekids.com
www.thomasandfriends.com
Printed in the United States of America
10 9 8 7 6 5 4 3 2 1

HiT entertainment

On the Island of Sodor, Sir Topham Hatt is building a new branch line for his railway.

It takes a big team to build a new branch line.

Marion meets Rex, Bert, and Mike,
three very small supply engines.

But Thomas believes that his branch line is still the most important one.

Cheeky Thomas races Gordon and derails his coaches.

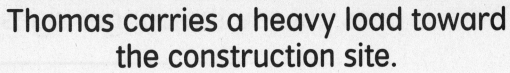

Thomas carries a heavy load toward the construction site.

Thomas does not see the danger signs.

Stop, Thomas, stop!

A crack widens! A hole opens up under the tracks!

Oh, no! Thomas is falling through!

Thomas falls into a cavern.

In the cavern, Thomas sees
something amazing.

Thomas has found a lost pirate ship!

The ship is sent by rail to Arlesburgh Harbor.

Mysterious strangers are excited to see the pirate ship.

That night, Henry thinks he sees a ghost!

The next day, Henry tells his friends.
No one believes him—except Salty!

Salty tells the story of the Lost Pirate . . .

Long ago, the Lost Pirate sailed the seas, stealing treasure from other ships.

The Lost Pirate hid his ship in a secret cove so he wouldn't be captured.

© Gullane (Thomas) LLC

Then the Lost Pirate buried his
stolen treasure.

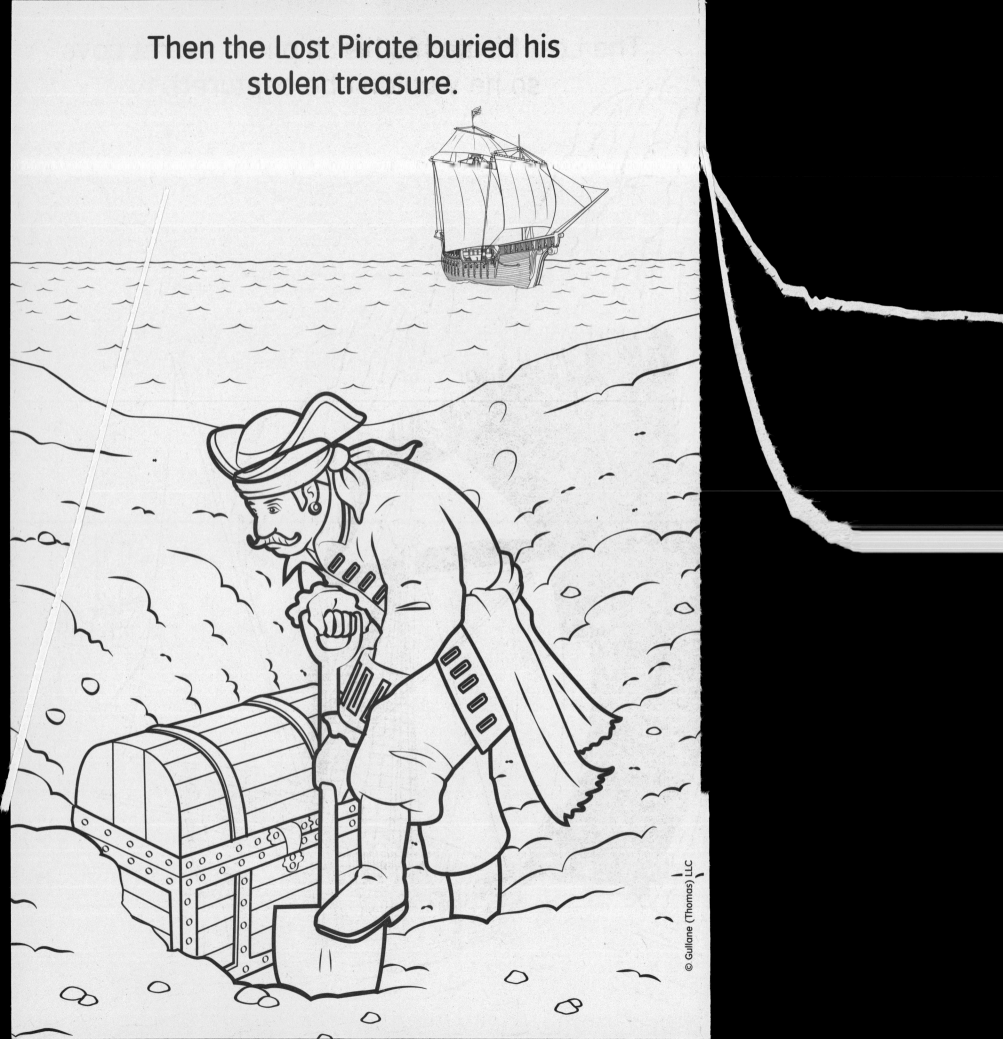

The Lost Pirate drew a map. He marked it with an X to show where the treasure was hidden. Salty's story ends.

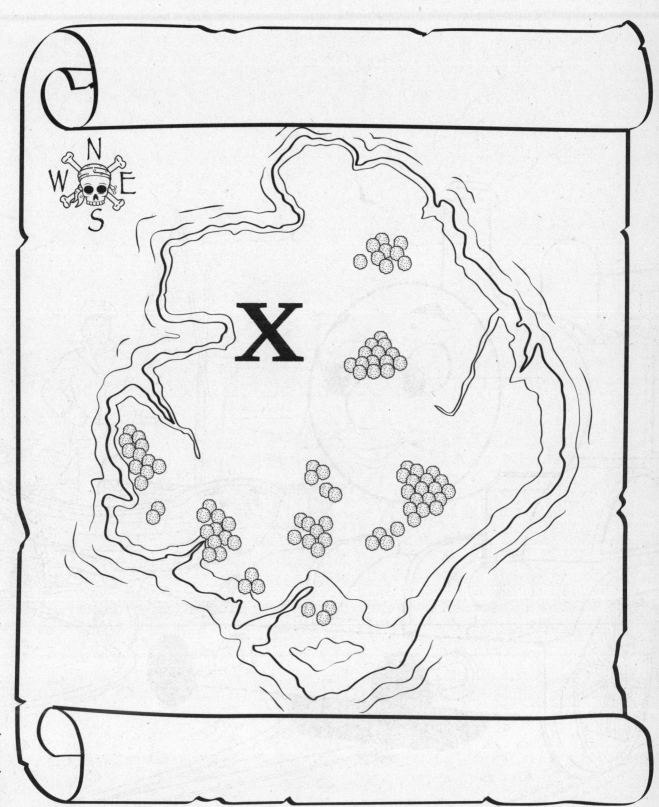

One night, Thomas meets Sailor John
and Skiff, a boat on wheels.

Thomas helps Sailor John explore the cavern.

Sailor John discovers the lost treasure map.
There really is buried treasure!

Thomas and Skiff become friends.

Ryan delivers dynamite to the construction
site. Sparks from his funnel start a fire.

Thomas pushes the burning trucks into the cavern. *Boom!*

Later, Marion finds the buried treasure chest!

Sailor John steals the treasure from Sir Topham Hatt's office.

Thomas chases Sailor John and Skiff, but he can't catch them!

Sailor John hitches Skiff to the pirate ship and speeds off again.

Thomas falls into the sea!
He is rescued.

Finally, Sailor John is captured!

The treasure is saved!

Remember that Thomas has to stay on the tracks until he reaches the station, and Skiff must stay in the stream until he reaches the pond behind the station!

FINISH

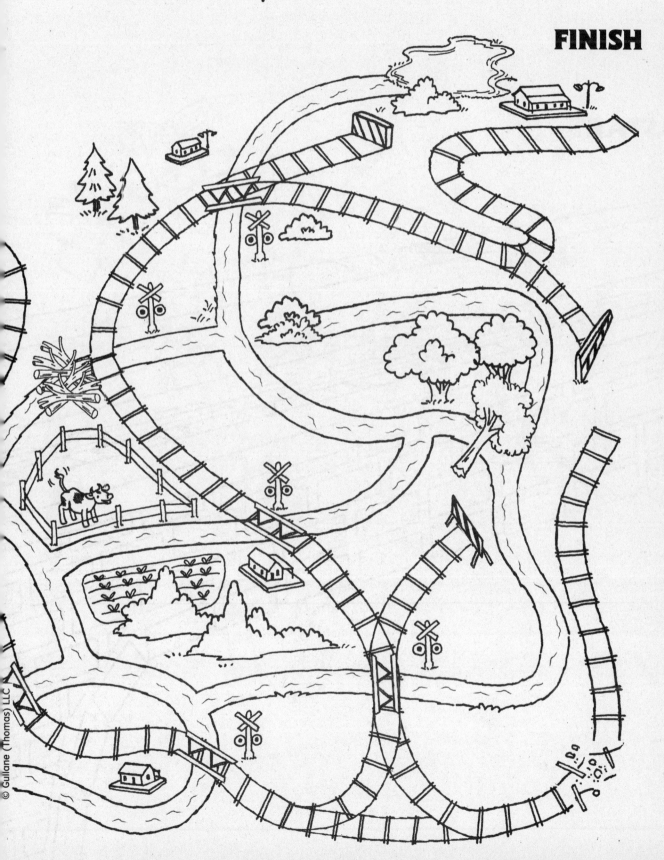

Draw Skiff as he races under the bridge.
Draw Thomas on the bridge.